MY FIRST ASSIGNMENT

A May Iverson Story

Elizabeth Jordan

first published in

1914

The Commencement exercises at St. Catharine's were over, and everybody in the big assembly-hall was looking relieved and grateful. Mabel Muriel Murphy had welcomed our parents and friends to the convent shades in an extemporaneous speech we had overheard her practising for weeks;

and the proud face of Mabel Muriel's father, beaming on her as she talked, illumined the front row like an electric globe. Maudie Joyce had read a beautiful essay, full of uplifting thoughts and rare flowers of rhetoric; Mabel Blossom had tried to deliver her address without the manuscript, and had forgotten it at a vital point; Adeline Thurston had recited an original poem; Kittie James had sung a solo; and Janet Trelawney had played the Sixth Hungarian Rhapsody on the piano.

Need I say who read the valedictory? It was I—May Iverson—winner of the Cross of Honor, winner of the Crown, leader of the convent orchestra, and president of the senior class. If there are those who think I should not mention these honors I will merely ask who would do it if I did not—and pause for a reply. Besides, young as I am, I know full well that worldly ambitions and triumphs are as ashes on the lips;

and already I was planning to cast mine aside. But at this particular minute the girls were crying on one another over our impending parting, and our parents were coming up to us and saying the same things again and again, while Sister Edna was telling Mabel Muriel Murphy, without being asked, that she was not ashamed of one of us.

I could see my father coming toward me through the crowd, stopping to shake hands with my classmates and tell them how wonderful they were; and I knew that when he reached me I must take him out into the convent garden and break his big, devoted heart. At the thought of it a great lump came into my throat, and while I was trying to swallow it I felt his arm flung over my shoulder.

He bent down and kissed me. "Well, my girl," he said, "I'm proud of you."

That was all. I knew it was all he would ever say; but it

meant more than any one else could put into hours of talk. I did not try to answer, but I kissed him hard, and, taking his arm, led him down-stairs, through the long halls and out into the convent garden, lovely with the scent of roses and honeysuckle and mignonette. He had never seen the garden before.

He wanted to stroll through it and glance into the conservatories, to look at the fountain and visit the Grotto of Lourdes and stand gazing up at the huge cross that rises from a bed of passion-flowers. But at last I took him into a little arbor and made him sit down. I was almost glad my delicate mother had not been able to come to see me graduate. He would tell her what I had to say better than I could.

When I have anything before me that is very hard I always want to do it immediately and get it over. So now I stood with my back braced against the side of the arbor, and, looking my dear father straight in the eyes, I told him I had made up my mind to be a nun.

At first he looked as if he thought I must be joking. Then, all in a minute, he seemed to change from a gallant middle-aged officer into a crushed, disappointed old man. He bowed his head, his shoulders sagged down, and, turning his eyes as if to keep me from seeing what was in them, he stared out over the convent garden.

"Why, May!" he said; and then again, very quietly, "Why, May!"

I told him all that was in my mind, and he listened without a word. At the end he said he had thought

I wanted to be a newspaper woman. I admitted that I had felt that desire a year ago—when I was only seventeen and my mind was immature. He sat up in his seat then and looked more comfortable—and younger.

"I'll put my answer in a nutshell," he said. "You're too

young still to know your mind about anything. Give your family and the world a chance. I don't want you to be a nun. I don't want you to be a newspaper woman, either. But I'll compromise. Be a newspaper woman for three years."

I began to speak, but he stopped me. "It's an interesting life," he went on. "You'll like it. But if you come to us the day you are twenty-one and tell us you still want to be a nun I promise that your mother and I will consent. Give us a chance, May." And he added, gently, "Play fair."

Those two words hurt; but they conquered me. I

agreed to do as he asked, and then we sat together, hand in hand, talking over plans, till the corners of the garden began to look mysterious in the twilight. Before we went back to the assembly-room it was understood that I was to go to New York in a week and begin my new career. Papa had friends there who would look after me.

I was sure they would never have a chance; but I did not mention that to my dear father then, while he was still feeling the shock of decision.

When I was saying good-by to Sister Irmingarde six days later I asked her to give me some advice about my newspaper work. "Write of things as they are," she said, without hesitation, "and write of them as simply as you can."

I was a little disappointed. I had expected something inspiring—something in the nature of a trumpet-call. I suppose she saw my face fall, for she smiled her beautiful smile.

"And when you write the sad stories you're so fond of, dear May," she said, "remember to let your readers shed their own tears."

I thought a great deal about those enigmatic words on my journey to New York, but after I reached it I forgot them. It was just as well, for no one associated with my work there had time to shed tears.

My editor was Mr. Nestor Hurd, of the *Searchlight*. He had promised to give me a trial because Kittie James's brother-in-law, George Morgan, who was his most intimate friend, said he must; but I don't think he really wanted to. When I reported to him he looked as if he had not eaten or slept for weeks, and as if seeing me was the one extra trouble he simply could not endure. There was a bottle of tablets on his desk, and every time he noticed it he stopped to swallow a tablet. He must have taken six while he was talking to me. He was a big man, with a round, smooth face, and dimples in his cheeks and chin. He talked out of one side of his mouth in a kind of low snarl, without looking at any one while he spoke.

"Oh," was his greeting to me, "you're the convent girl? Ready for work? All right. I'll try you on this."

He turned to the other person in the office—a thin young man at a desk near him. Neither of them had risen when I entered.

"Here, Morris," he said. "Put Miss Iverson down for the Ferncliff story."

The young man called Morris dropped a big pencil and looked

very much surprised.

"But—" he said.
"Why, say, she'll
have to stay out in
that house alone—all
night."

Mr. Hurd said shortly
that I couldn't be in a
safer place. "Are you
afraid of ghosts?"
he asked, without
looking at me. I said
I was not, and waited
for him to explain

the joke; but he didn't.

"Here's the story," he said. "Listen, and get it straight. Ferncliff is a big country house out on Long Island, about three miles from Sound View. It's said to be haunted. Its nearest neighbor is a quarter of a mile away. It was empty for three years until this spring. Last month Mrs. Wallace Vanderveer, a New York society woman, took a year's lease of it and moved in with a lot of servants. Last week she moved out. Servants wouldn't stay. Said they heard noises and saw ghosts. She heard noises, too. Now the owner of Ferncliff, a Miss Watts, is suing Mrs. Vanderveer for a year's rent. Nice little story in it. See it?"

I didn't, exactly. That is, I didn't see what he wanted me to do about it, and I said so.

"I want you to take the next train for Sound View," he snarled, impatiently, and pulled the left side of his mouth

down to his chin.
"When you get there,
drive out and look
at Ferncliff to see
what it's like in the
daytime. Then go
to the Sound View
Hotel and have your
dinner. About ten
o'clock go back to
Ferncliff, and stay
there all night.
Sit up. If you see
any ghosts, write
about 'em. If you
don't, write about

how it felt to stay there and wait for 'em. Come back to town to-morrow morning and turn in your story. If it's good we'll run it. If it isn't," he added, grimly, "we'll throw it out. See now?" I saw now.

"Here's the key of the house," he said. "We got it from the agent." He turned and began to talk to Mr. Morris about something else— and I knew that our interview was over.

I went to Sound View on the first train, and drove straight from the station to Ferncliff. It was almost five o'clock, and a big storm was coming up. The rain was like a wet, gray veil, and the wind snarled in the tops of the pine-trees in a way that made me think of Mr. Hurd. I didn't like the look of the house. It was a huge, gloomy, vine-covered place, perched on a bluff overlooking the Sound, and set far back from the road. An avenue of pines led up to it, and a high box-hedge along the front cut off the grounds from the road and the near-by fields. When we drove away my cabman kept glancing back over his shoulder as if he expected to see the ghosts.

I was glad to get into the hotel and have a few hours for thought. I was already perfectly sure that I was not going to like being a newspaper woman, and I made up my mind to write to papa the next morning and tell him so. I thought of the convent and of Sister Irmingarde, who was probably at vespers now in the chapel, and the idea of that assignment became more unpleasant every minute. Not that I was afraid—I, an Iverson, and the daughter of a general in the army! But the thing seemed silly and unworthy of a convent girl, and lonesome work besides. As I thought of the convent it suddenly seemed so near that I could almost hear its vesper bell, and that comforted me.

I went back to

Ferncliff at ten o'clock. By that time the storm was really wild. It might have been a night in November instead of in July. The house looked very bleak and lonely, and the way my driver lashed his horse and hurried away from the neighborhood did not make it easier for me to unlock the front door and go in. But I forced myself to do it.

I had filled a basket with candles and matches and some books and a good luncheon, which the landlady at the hotel had put up for me. I hurriedly lighted two candles and locked the front door. Then I took the candles into the living-room at the left of the hall, and set them on a table. They made two little blurs of light in which the linen-covered furniture assumed queer, ghostly shapes that seemed to move as the flames flickered. I did not like the effect, so I lighted some more candles.

I was sure the first duty of a reporter was to search the

house. So I took a candle in each hand and went into every room, up stairs and down, spending a great deal of time in each, for it was strangely comforting to be busy. I heard all sorts of sounds— mice in the walls, old boards cracking under my feet, and a death-tick that began to get on my nerves, though I knew what it was. But there was nothing more than might be heard in any other old house.

When I returned to the living-room I looked at my luncheon-basket— not that I was hungry, but I wanted something more to do, and eating would have filled the time so pleasantly. But if I ate, there would be nothing to look forward to but the ghost, so I decided to wait. Outside, the screeching wind seemed to be sweeping the rain before it in a rising fury. It was half past eleven. Twelve is the hour when ghosts are said to come, I remembered.

I took up a book and began to read. I had

almost forgotten my surroundings when a noise sounded on the veranda, a noise that made me stop reading to listen. Something was out there—something that tried the knob of the door and pushed against the panels; something that scampered over to the window-blinds and pulled at them; something that opened the shutters and tried to peer in.

I laid down my book. The feet scampered back to the door. I stopped breathing. There followed a knocking at the door, the knocking of weak hands, which soon began to beat against the panels with closed fists; and next I heard a high, shrill voice. It seemed to be calling, uttering words, but above the shriek of the storm I could not make out what they were.

Creeping along the floor to the window, I pulled back one of the heavy curtains and raised the green shade under it half an inch. For a moment I could see nothing but the twisting pines.

But at last I was able to distinguish something moving near the door— something no larger than a child, but with white hair floating round its head. It was not a ghost. It was not an animal. It could not be a human being. I had no idea what it was. While I looked it turned and came toward the window where I was crouching, as if it felt my eyes upon it. And this time I heard its words.

"Let me in!" it shrieked. "Let me in! Let me in!" And in a kind of fury it scampered back and dashed itself against the door.

Then I was afraid—not merely nervous—afraid—with

a degrading fear that made my teeth chatter. If only I had known what it was; if only I could think of something normal that was a cross between a little child and an old woman! I went to the door and noiselessly turned the key. I meant to open it an inch and ask what was there. But almost before the door had moved on its hinges the thing outside saw it. It gave a quick spring and a little screech and threw itself against the panels. The next instant I went back and down, and the thing that had been outside was inside.

I got up slowly and looked at it. It seemed to be a witch—a little old, humpbacked witch—not more than four feet high, with white hair that hung in wet locks around a shriveled brown face, and black eyes gleaming at me in the dark hall like an angry cat's.

"You little fool!" she hissed. "Why didn't you let me in? I'm soaked through. And why didn't that bell ring? What's been done to the wire?"

I could not speak, and after looking at me a moment more the little old creature locked the hall door and walked into the living-room, motioning to me to follow. She was panting with anger or exhaustion, or both. When we had entered the room she turned and grinned at me like a malicious monkey.

"Scared you, didn't I?" she chuckled, in her high, cracked voice. "Serves you right. Keeping me out on that veranda fifteen minutes!"

She began to gather up the loose locks of her white hair and fasten them at the back of her head. "Wind blew me to pieces," she muttered.

She took off her long black coat, threw it over a chair, and straightened the hat that hung over one ear. She was a human being, after all; a terribly deformed human being, whose great, hunched back now showed distinctly through her plain black dress. There was a bit of lace at her throat, and when she took off her gloves handsome rings glittered on her claw-like fingers.

"Well, well," she said, irritably, "don't stand there staring. I know I'm not a beauty," and she cackled like an angry hen.

But it was reassuring, at least, to know she was human, and I felt myself getting warm again. Then, as she seemed to expect me to say something, I explained that I had not intended to let anybody in, because I thought nobody had any right in the house.

"Humph," she said. "I've got a better

right here than you have, young lady. I am the owner of this house and everything in it—I am Miss Watts. And I'll tell you one thing"—she suddenly began to trot around the room—"I've stood this newspaper nonsense about ghosts just as long as I'm going to. It's ruining the value of my property. I live in

Brooklyn, but when my agent telephoned me to-night that a reporter was out here working up another lying yarn I took the first train and came here to protect my interests."

She grumbled something about having sent her cab away at the gate and having mislaid her keys. I asked her if she meant to stay till morning, and she glared at me and snapped that she certainly did. Then, taking a candle, she wandered off by herself for a while, and I heard her scampering around on the upper floors. When she came back she seemed very much surprised to hear that I was not going to bed.

"You're a fool," she said, rudely, "but I suppose you've got to do what the other fools tell you to."

After that I didn't feel much like sharing my supper with her, but I did, and she seemed to enjoy it. Then she curled herself up on a big divan in the corner and grinned at me again. I liked her face better when she was angry.

"I'm going to take a nap," she said. "Call me if any ghosts come."

I opened my book again and read for half an hour. Then suddenly, from somewhere under the house, I heard a queer, muffled sound. "Tap, tap, tap," it went. And again, "Tap, tap, tap."

At first it didn't interest me much. But after a minute I realized that it was different from anything I had heard that night. And soon another noise mingled with it—a kind of buzz, like the whir of an electric fan, only louder. I looked at Miss Watts. She was asleep.

I picked up a candle and followed the noise—through the hall, down the cellar steps, and along a bricked passage. There the sound stopped. I stood still and waited. While I was staring at the bricks in front of me I noticed one that seemed to have a light behind it. I lowered my candle and examined it. Some plaster had been knocked out, and through a hole the size of a penny I saw another passage cutting through the earth like a little catacomb, with a light at the far end of it. While I was staring, amazed, the tapping began again, much nearer now; and I heard men's voices.

There were men under that house, in a secret cellar!

In half a minute I was standing beside Miss Watts, shaking her arm and trying to wake her. Almost before I was able to make her understand what I had seen she was through the front door and half-way down the avenue, dragging me with her.

"Where are we going?" I gasped.

"To the next house, idiot, to telephone to the police," she said. "Do you think we could stay there and do it?"

We left the avenue and came into the road, and as we ran on, stumbling into mud-holes and whipped by wind and rain, she panted out that the men were probably escaped convicts from some prison or patients from some asylum. I ran faster after that, though I hadn't thought I could. I wondered if I were having a bad dream. Several times I pinched myself, but I didn't wake up. Instead, I kept on running and stumbling and gasping, until I felt sure I had been running and stumbling and gasping for years and must keep on doing it for eons more. But at last we came to a house set far back in big grounds, and we raced side by side up the driveway that led to the front door. Late as it was, there were lights everywhere, and through the long windows opening on the veranda we could see people moving about.

Miss Watts gave the bell a terrific pull; some one opened the door, and we stumbled in. After that everything was a mixture of questions and answers and excitement and telephoning, followed by a long wait for the police. A man led Miss Watts and me into a room where a fire was burning, and left us to get warm and dry. When we were alone I asked Miss Watts if she thought they would keep us overnight. She stared at me.

"You won't have

much time for sleep," she answered, almost kindly. "It will take you an hour or two to write your story."

It was my turn to stare, and I did it. "My story?" I asked her. "To-night? What do you mean?"

She swung round in her chair and stared at me harder than ever. Then she cackled in her nastiest way. "And this is a New York reporter!" she said. "Why, you little dunce, you know you've got a story, don't you?"

"Yes," I answered, doubtfully. "But I'm to write it to-morrow, after I talk to Mr. Hurd."

Miss Watts uttered a

squawk and then a squeal. "I don't know what fool sent you here," she snapped, "or what infant-class you've escaped from. But one thing I do know: You came here to write a Sunday 'thriller,' I suppose, which would have destroyed what little value my property has left. By bull-headed luck you've stumbled on the truth; and it's a good news story. It will please your editor, and it will save my property. Now, here's my point." She pushed her horrible little face close to mine and kept it there while she finished. "That story is coming out in the *Searchlight* to-morrow morning. I'd do it if I could, but I'm not a writer. So you're going to write it and telephone it in to the *Searchlight* office within the next hour. Have I made myself clear?"

She had. I felt my face getting red and hot when I realized that I had a big story and had not known it. I wondered if I could ever live that down. I felt so humble that I was almost willing to let Miss Watts see it.

But before I could answer her there was the noise of many feet in the hall, with the voices of men. Then our door was flung open, and a young man came in, wearing a rain-coat, thick boots covered with mud, and a wide grin. He was saving time by shaking the rain off his soft hat as he crossed the room to us. His eyes touched me, then passed on to Miss Watts as if I hadn't been there.

"Miss Watts," he said, "the police are here, and I'm going back to the house with them to see the capture. I'm Gibson, of the *Searchlight*."

Miss Watts actually

smiled at him. Then she held out her skinny little claw of a hand. "A real reporter!" she said. "Thank Heaven! You know what it means to me to have this thing put straight. But how do you happen to be here?"

"Hurd sent me to look after Miss Iverson," he explained, glancing at me again. "He couldn't put her in a haunted house without a watch-dog, but, to do her justice, she didn't know she had one. I was in a summer-house on the grounds. I saw you leave and followed you here. Then I went up the road to meet the police."

He grinned at me,

and I smiled a very little smile in return. I wasn't going to give him a whole smile until I found out how he was going to act about my story. Miss Watts started for the door.

"Come on," she said, with her hand on the knob.

The real reporter's eyes grew big. "Are

you going along?" he gasped.

"Certainly I'm going along," snapped Miss Watts. "I'm going to see this thing through. And I'll tell you one thing right now, young man," she ended, "if you don't put the facts into your story I'm going to sue your newspaper for twenty-five thousand dollars."

He did not answer. His attention seemed to be diverted to me. I was standing beside Miss Watts, buttoning my rain-coat and pulling my hat over my eyes again, preparatory to going out.

"Say, kid," said the real reporter, "you go back and sit down.

You're not in this, you know. We'll come and get you and take you to the hotel after it's all over."

I gave him a cold and dignified glance. Then I buttoned the last button of my coat and went out into the hall. It was full of men. The real reporter hurried after me. He seemed to expect me to say

something. So finally
I did.

"Mr. Hurd told me
to write this story,"
I explained, in level
tones, "and I'm going
to try to write it. And
I can't write it unless
I see everything that
happens."

I looked at him and
Miss Watts out of the
corner of my eye as I
spoke, and I distinctly

saw them give each other a significant glance. Miss Watts shrugged her shoulders as if she didn't care what I did; but the real reporter looked worried.

"Oh, well, all right," he said, at last. "I suppose it isn't fair not to let you in on your own assignment. There's one good thing—you can't get any wetter and muddier than you are." That thought seemed to comfort him.

We had a hard time going back, but it was easier because there were more of us to suffer. Besides, the real reporter helped Miss Watts and me a little when we stumbled or when the wind blew us against a tree or a fence. When we got near the house everybody moved very quietly, keeping close to the high hedge. We all went around to the back entrance. There the chief constable began to give his men orders, and the real reporter led Miss Watts and me into a grape-arbor, about fifty feet from the house.

"This is where we've got to stay," he whispered, pulling us inside and closing the door. "We can see them come out, and get the other details from Conroy, who's in charge."

The police were creeping closer to the house. Three of them took places outside while the rest went forward. First there was a long silence; then a sudden rush and crash—shouts and words that we didn't catch. Gleams of light flashed up for a minute— then disappeared. The men stationed outside the house ran toward the cellar. There was the flashing of more light, and at last the police came out with their prisoners—and the whole thing was over. There had not been a pistol-shot.

I was as warm as toast in my wet clothes, but my teeth were chattering with excitement, and I knew Miss Watts was excited, too, by the grip of her hand on my shoulder. The men came toward us through the rain on their way to the gate, and Mr. Conroy's voice sounded as if he had been running a race. But he hadn't. He had been right there.

"Well, Miss Watts, we've got 'em," he crowed. "A nice little gang of amachur counterfeiters. They've been visitin' you for 'most a year, snug and cozy; but I guess this is the end of your troubles."

Miss Watts walked out into the rain and, taking a policeman's electric bull's-eye, looked at the prisoners one by one. I followed her and looked, too, while the real reporter talked to Mr. Conroy. There were three counterfeiters, and they were all handcuffed and looked young. It could not have been very hard for six policemen to take them. One of them had blood on his face, and another was covered with mud, as if he had been rolled in it. Miss Watts asked the bloody one, who was also the biggest one, if his gang had really worked in a secret cellar at Ferncliff for a year. He said it had been there about ten months.

"Then you were there all winter?" Miss Watts asked him. "And you were so safe and comfortable that when the tenants moved in and you found they were all women, except a stupid butler, you decided to scare them away and stay right along?"

The man muttered something that seemed to mean that she was right. The real reporter interrupted, looking busy and worried again. "Miss Watts," he said, quickly, "can't we go right into your house and send this story to the *Searchlight* over your telephone? It's a quarter to one, and there isn't a minute to lose. The *Searchlight* goes to press in an hour. I've got all the facts," he added, in a peaceful tone.

Miss Watts said we could, and led the way into the house, while the counterfeiters and the police tramped off through the mud and rain. When we got inside, Miss Watts took us to the library and lit the electric lights, while the real reporter bustled about, looking busier than any one I ever saw before. I watched him for a minute. Then I told Miss Watts I wanted to go into a quiet room and write my story. She and the real reporter looked at each other again. I was getting tired of their looks. The real reporter spoke to me very kindly, like a Sunday-school superintendent addressing his class.

"Now, see here, Miss Iverson," he said; "you've had a big, new experience and lots of excitement. You discovered the counterfeiters.

You'll get full credit for it. Let it go at that, and I'll write the story. It's got to be a real story, not a kindergarten special."

If he hadn't said that about the kindergarten special I might have let him write the story, for I was cold and tired and scared. But at those fatal words I felt myself stiffen all over.

"It's my story," I said, with icy determination. "And I'm going to write it."

The real reporter looked annoyed. "But can you?" he protested. "We haven't time for experiments."

"Of course I can," I said. And I'm afraid I

spoke crossly, for I was getting annoyed. "I'll write it exactly the way Sister Irmingarde told me to."

I sat down at the table as I spoke. I heard a bump and something that sounded like a groan. The real reporter had fallen into a chair. "Good Lord!" he said; and then for a long time he didn't say anything. Finally he began to fuss with his paper, as if he meant to write the story anyway. I wrote three pages and forgot about him. At last he muttered, "Here, let me see those," and his voice sounded like a dove's when it mourns under the eaves. I pushed the sheets toward him with my left hand

and went on writing. Suddenly I heard a gasp and a chuckle. In another second the real reporter was standing beside me, grinning his widest grin.

"Why, say, you little May Iverson kid," he almost shouted, "this story is going to be good!"

I could hear Miss

Watts straighten up in the chair from which she was watching us. She snatched at my pages, and he let her have them. I wanted to draw myself up to my full height and look at him coldly, but I didn't—there wasn't time. Besides, far down inside of me I was delighted by his praise.

"Of course it's going to be good," was all I said. "Sister Irmingarde told me to write about things as they are, and very simply."

He had my pages back in his hands now and was running over them quickly, putting in a few words here and there with a pencil. I could see he was not changing much. Then he started on a jump for the next room, where the telephone was, but stopped at the door. There was a queer look in his eyes.

"Sister Irmingarde's a daisy!" he muttered.

Then I heard him calling New York. "Gimme the *Searchlight*," he called. "Gimme the city desk. Hurry up! Say, Jack, this is Gibson, at Sound View. We've got a crackerjack of a story out here. No— the Iverson kid is doing it. It's all right, too. Get Hammond busy there and let him take it on the typewriter as fast as I read it. Ready? Here goes."

He began to read my first page.

Miss Watts got up and shut the door, and I bowed my thanks to her. The storm was worse than ever, but I hardly heard it. For a second his words had made me think of Sister Irmingarde. I felt sorry for her. She would never have a chance like this—to write a real news story for a great newspaper. The convent seemed like a place I had heard of, long ago.

Then I settled down to work, and for the next hour there was no sound in the room but the whisper of my busy pen and the respectful footsteps of Miss Watts as she reverently carried my story, page by page, to the chastened "real reporter."

ABOUT THE AUTHOR

Elizabeth Jordan was born in Milwaukee, Wisconsin in 1865. After working in the local papers she moved to New York City in 1890 and joined the staff of Joseph Pulitzer's *The New York World*. Her column, "True Stories of the News" chronicled everyday life in the city.

ABOUT THE COVER

The image on the cover is adapted from a photograph of typewriter in Santiago, Chile taken by McKay Savage.

MAY IVERSON
RETURNS IN
*THE CRY OF
THE PACK*

MORE BOOKS AT:

superlargeprint.com

KEEP ON READING!

ISBN 9781790586769

Made in the
USA
Columbia, SC